Super Special #3

The Case of
the
Missing Falcon

Read all the Jigsaw Jones Mysteries

And Don't Miss . . .

Coming Soon . . .

Super Special #3

The Case of the Missing Falcon

by James Preller
illustrated by Jamie Smith
cover illustration by R. W. Alley

A
LITTLE APPLE
PAPERBACK

SCHOLASTIC INC.
New York Toronto London Auckland Sydney
Mexico City New Delhi Hong Kong Buenos Aires

In this, the twenty-fifth Jigsaw Jones book (Super Special #3, plus #s 1–22 in the regular series), I decided to pay tribute to two great writers of hard-boiled detective fiction, by way of thanks.

This book is dedicated to the classic 1929 detective novel, Dashiell Hammett's The Maltese Falcon, *which I used as source and inspiration for* The Case of the Missing Falcon.

In addition, the opening chapter of this book mirrors the first scene of Raymond Chandler's The Little Sister. *Just for kicks.*

Apologies to any fly lovers in the house.

— J.P.

No part of this publication may be reproduced in whole or in part, or stored in a retrieval system, or transmitted in any form or by any means, electronic, mechanical, photocopying, recording, or otherwise, without written permission of the publisher. For information regarding permission, write to Scholastic Inc., Attention: Permissions Department, 557 Broadway, New York, NY 10012.

ISBN 0-439-55997-9

Text copyright © 2004 by James Preller. Illustrations copyright © 2004 by Scholastic Inc. All rights reserved. Published by Scholastic Inc. SCHOLASTIC, LITTLE APPLE PAPERBACKS, A JIGSAW JONES MYSTERY, and associated logos are trademarks and/or registered trademarks of Scholastic Inc.

12 11 10 9 8 7 6 5   5 6 7 8 9/0

Printed in the U.S.A.   40
First printing, January 2004

CONTENTS

Chapter One
The Fly

There's a hand-lettered sign behind an old desk in my basement. It reads: JIGSAW JONES, PRIVATE EYE. I solve mysteries. Lost dogs, missing coins, stolen baseball cards — that kind of thing. If somebody loses a pet parakeet, they usually come squawking to me. I rarely turn down a case. I'll do just about anything to solve a mystery, as long as it's honest.

I was sitting at my desk, studying the pieces of an "I Spy" jigsaw puzzle,

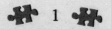 1

wondering whether the white piece I had in my hand belonged to a fluffy cloud, a bunny rabbit, or a white horse. A phone sat on the corner of the desk, offering no help at all.

A fly buzzed around my head. I slowly reached for the swatter and waited. From the small basement window a beam of light spilled across the desk. I knew that, sooner or later, that's where the fly would land. I

was all set and ready to go. Instead, the fly seemed happy to do rollovers, dives, and loop-dee-loops. Then the buzzing stopped. And there he was.

The phone rang. I reached for it slowly and whispered, "Jigsaw Jones, Private Eye. Please hold."

I blinked once and swung. The poor guy never knew what hit him. He bounced, popped into the air, and fell to the ground. I picked him up by a wing, tossed him into my New York Mets garbage can, and returned to the phone.

"Thanks for holding," I said. "How can I help you?"

A girl's voice answered. "Hi . . . um . . . you're the second-grader who's a detective, right?"

"Right."

"How much do you charge?" she asked.

"It depends on the job," I answered. "What have you got in mind?"

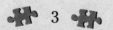

She paused. "I don't think that . . . well . . . it's hard to explain over the phone."

"Try," I said.

"Somebody has something of mine . . ." she told me. "Maybe."

"Maybe," I repeated. "Or maybe it's just a wild-goose chase."

She sighed into the phone.

I thought about my pockets. I thought about how they were empty. And how I wouldn't mind having a few dollars to fill them up.

"Hey," I said cheerfully. "For a dollar a day, I'll chase a wild goose. I'll even wrestle an alligator. Why don't you come to my office and we'll talk about it?"

"No . . . no . . . I can't," she insisted. "You come here."

I suddenly realized where the white puzzle piece went. It was part of the white knight. He was rescuing a princess from a dragon, though it looked like he might need a little help. I snapped the piece into place. "Tell me where *here* is," I replied, "and I'll be right *there*."

Chapter Two
Elana Wonderly

My partner, Mila Yeh, and I parked our bikes at 17 Penny Lane. There was a garage sale going on. The driveway was lined with folding tables that were filled with all sorts of junk that nobody wanted. There were ashtrays that looked like ducks, old toys with missing parts in battered boxes, milk crates overflowing with chewed-up paperback books.

There were clothes, too: tattered T-shirts, bathrobes, acid-washed jeans. I dragged Mila away from a pile of used shoes. "Come

on," I said. "I think that's her behind the picnic table."

"Gosh, she's cute," Mila gushed.

I groaned unhappily.

Elana Wonderly had dark red hair, and a lot of it. She wore a tight print shirt that crept up over her belly button. Her jeans flared at the bottom, with flower designs stenciled on them. I noticed her eyes right away. They were green as emeralds and cold as ice.

I handed her my card:

NEED A MYSTERY SOLVED?
Call Jigsaw Jones
or Mila Yeh!
For a dollar a day,
we make problems go away.

CALL 555-4523 or 555-4374

Elana sat down on the edge of a chair, holding the card in her lap. She chewed on her lower lip like it was a piece of bubble gum.

Two women stood nearby, talking about an antique lamp. One of them had the same long legs and the same dark red hair as Elana Wonderly. "Is this a good place to talk?" I asked. "Or do we need to go somewhere private?"

Elana pulled on her lower lip. She was giving it quite a workout. An idea seemed to form behind her eyes.

"Mother," she called out, "can you make me some lunch? I'll watch the cash box."

Elana's mother smiled. "Sure thing, Princess! How about your favorite, a fluffer-nutter sandwich?"

"Thank you, Mother," Elana said, a little too politely. "And chocolate milk, too, but not too chocolatey." After a pause she added, "Pretty please!"

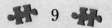 9

With her mother busy inside the house, Elana reached into the cash box, counted out five dollars, and handed them to me.

"Five dollars is a lot of money," I said.

"I need your help, and I'm desperate," Elana said, ignoring Mila and looking directly at me. "I hear you're the best."

"I have good days and bad days," I

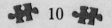

answered with a shrug. "Where did you hear about me?"

Elana blinked twice. Her eyes grew moist, like wet jewels. "There's been an awful mistake. I . . . I . . . didn't know what to do!" she sobbed.

"It's not always easy to know what to do," Mila commented.

"That's right," I agreed, watching Elana dab her eyes with a tissue. "Tell us about it, from the beginning. Then maybe we'll know what needs doing."

Chapter Three

Trust

"How can I be sure I can trust you?" Elana asked.

"You just gave me five pictures of a dead president," I said, patting the dollar bills in my pocket. "It seems like you trust me already."

Elana smiled, flashing a long row of white teeth. Her eyes twinkled at mine. I dug my hands in my pockets and waited. I don't think my eyes twinkled back.

She brushed away a strand of hair.

"You're good," she said. "I can see I'm going to like you . . . very much."

My hands began to sweat.

Mila interrupted. "Can you tell us exactly what happened?"

Elana shot Mila a quick dark look, then made her face sunny again. She spoke only to me. "Something was taken that shouldn't have been. I'm afraid it may have been my fault."

"Taken?" I asked. "Or stolen?"

"I'm not sure," she answered. "I was supposed to be right here, watching things, but I was inside at the time."

"Inside the house?" I asked. "Why?"

Elana blushed. "I'd rather not say."

Mila pulled on her long black hair. "Start from the beginning," she urged.

Again, Elana ignored Mila. She spoke directly to me. "You see, we've been cleaning the house. Getting rid of old junk. The garage sale was my idea. But this stuff

back here" — she pointed toward the back of the garage — "wasn't supposed to be for sale."

I nodded.

"There was a small statue . . . a falcon. It was my brother's . . . and I took it down to look at it," she told me. "I guess I left it here on the table without thinking."

"And when you came back from inside," I said, "the statue was gone."

Elana picked at a fingernail. She glanced nervously at the kitchen window, where her mother stood by the sink. Again she blinked twice before answering. "Yes, Jigsaw. It was gone."

Mila spoke up. "What's so special about this falcon?"

"I never said it was *special*," Elana snapped. "I said it was missing. And now I want it back. Isn't that enough?"

"But —" Mila began, angrily.

I cut Mila off. "Yeah, sure, it's missing

and you want it back. That's enough for us."

Somewhere in the distance a lawn mower started up. Elana's mother came out, carrying lunch on a silver tray. A maid could not have done it any smoother.

Elana frowned. "No straw, Mother?"

Mrs. Wonderly's shoulders sagged. "A straw? I'm sorry, Princess," she said. "I'll be right back."

In a hushed voice, Elana said, "I can't talk anymore."

I placed my hands on the table and leaned close to Elana Wonderly. I whispered, "We'll have a look around. I've got more questions, but I guess they can stand in line and wait like everybody else. In the meantime, make a list of suspects. Anybody who was here today who might have acted strangely. Anybody at all."

Elana grinned. She slipped my card into her back pocket. "I'll call you, Jigsaw."

"You can call me Jigsaw, or you can call me anything else you want," I replied. "Just get me that list." My joke flew over her head like a startled sparrow. "We'll ask around," I concluded. "Do a little snooping. Maybe dig something up."

"I hope so," Elana answered, eyes beaming at me again. Her lips curled into a sly smile. Then, just as suddenly, her eyes darkened. She shouted over her shoulder, "Mother! Where's that straw?!"

The day was winding down. There were only a few customers in sight, but no one suspicious. Mila and I poked around. I bought a few cheap baseball cards to make things look right to the mom. Then we got on our bikes and headed home.

"So, what did you think of her?" I asked Mila as we rode.

Mila paused, weighing her words. "You heard Elana's mother call her 'Princess.' That's what she is, Jigsaw. Very pretty. Very spoiled."

"I'm worried that she likes me," I answered glumly. "You saw the way she looked at me. It gave me the creeps."

Mila laughed. "No, Jigsaw. She's just *pretending* that she likes you."

"Pretending?" I asked. "How do you know?"

"A girl knows," Mila answered mysteriously.

"There's one more small problem," I added.

"What's that?"

I sped up on my bike, passing close to Mila.

"She's lying."

Chapter Four

I Don't Like Mondays

Monday was, well, Monday. It's not exactly my favorite day of the week. It meant school, which wasn't too bad. But it got in the way of detective work.

Our teacher was Ms. Gleason. She might be the best teacher in the solar system. But since I haven't visited Mars or Pluto lately, let's just say that Ms. Gleason is the nicest teacher I've ever had. And I've been around the block a few times.

Still, a detective can get a lot done in

school. There's a ton of people to talk to. If you ask enough questions, you usually get answers. By lunchtime, Mila had the scoop on Elana Wonderly. We talked over soggy cardboard plates of spaghetti and meatballs.

"She's a third-grader in Ms. Ali-Turay's class," Mila said. "Most of her friends are boys. To tell you the truth, it was hard to find a girl who had anything nice to say about her."

"That doesn't surprise you," I noted.

Mila shrugged. "I don't know, Jigsaw. I hate to think badly about anybody."

"She's not telling us the whole story," I said. "That's for sure."

"It sounded fishy," Mila agreed.

I widened my eyes and made fish lips. "Yeah, *glub-glub*."

"Did you notice how she changed the subject when I asked where she heard about me?" I asked.

Mila smiled. "Boo-hoo. Those tears were as fake as Monopoly money."

I smiled. "Elana blinked twice every time she lied. My neighbor Wingnut O'Brien used to pull on his ear. It's called 'the tell,'" I explained. "All liars do something to give themselves away."

"So what do we do now?" Mila wondered.

"Five dollars is a lot of money," I mused. "I guess we keep looking for the falcon . . . and hope we don't find a wild goose."

By afternoon recess, we had a list of kids from room 201 who said they went to the garage sale at 17 Penny Lane:

1. Kim Lewis
2. Athena Lorenzo
3. Eddie Becker
4. Danika Starling

It wasn't much. But it was a start.

"Are you sure that's everybody?" I double-checked with Mila.

"I'm sure," she said.

Of course, if somebody *did* steal the falcon, they probably wouldn't admit to being there. But now we had witnesses at the scene of the crime. Our list would get a lot longer before we were done.

Toward the end of the day, Ms. Gleason had us open our writing folders. She wrote the words CHARACTER, SETTING, and PLOT on an easel. "Who can remember what these are?" she asked.

Danika Starling reached for the ceiling. "A character is, um, like a person in a story," she answered.

"Very good, Danika. A character can be a person, or even an animal," Ms. Gleason added. "It could be a boy or a girl or even a rat, like Templeton in *Charlotte's Web*." She drew an arrow from the word CHARACTER and wrote, WHO.

Mila raised her hand. "Setting is where a story takes place," she said.

"That's right, Mila," Ms. Gleason said. She wrote WHERE next to the word SETTING. "We usually learn about setting through descriptive language. Words paint a picture for us. Words help us see what's going on."

"Like pictures on television," Eddie Becker said.

"Exactly," Ms. Gleason replied. "And how

about plot?" Ms. Gleason asked, looking around the room. "Anybody?"

"It's where somebody's buried!" shouted Bobby Solofsky.

"Well, yes," Ms. Gleason answered. "A plot in a graveyard. But in a story a plot is WHAT happens. For example, a girl in a store finds a ring. Character, setting, plot."

A <u>girl</u> in a <u>store</u> finds a ring.
          ↑   ↑
      character   setting   plot

The bus announcements came over the loudspeaker.

"Okay, boys and girls," Ms. Gleason said. "Put away your things. Tomorrow we'll read *Wemberly Worried* by Kevin Henkes. We'll work on making up our own characters."

And then we were saved by the bell.

Chapter Five

Fishier and Fishier

Mila and I had just started a game of Clue when Stringbean Noonan leaned on my doorbell.

Stringbean's real name was Jasper. We called him Stringbean because he was the skinniest kid in room 201. He was a nice kid, but very nervous. He was afraid of bees, and thunder, and pretty much anything that moved. He didn't care for sports. Instead, Stringbean spent most of his time staring through a telescope into space, dreaming about faraway places.

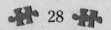

Go figure.

"Stringbean," I said. "What's up?"

Stringbean looked around nervously. "I need your help, Jigsaw," he said. "I'm in big trouble."

"Trouble is my business," I replied.

Mila and I led him to my tree house in the backyard. I poured three cups of grape juice. Then I opened my detective journal and listened.

"I lost something valuable," Stringbean told us in a rush of words. "Now my cousin is going to kill me. I knew I shouldn't have listened to her."

"Slow down, Stringbean," I said. "Nobody is going to kill anybody. What did you lose?"

"A statue," he answered.

"Say that again," I said.

"A statue . . . of a falcon," Stringbean repeated. "I hid it in a tree. And now it's gone."

Mila and I looked at each other in surprise. Mila asked, "Is it your falcon?"

Stringbean shook his head. "Well, not exactly. I mean, no, it's not mine. It's my cousin's, sort of."

"Sort of," I echoed gloomily.

"Tell us the whole story," Mila said.

"Yeah," I said. "Character, setting, plot — the works."

"It happened yesterday," Stringbean began. "My cousin Elana called me up."

Mila stopped him short. "Elana Wonderly, correct?"

"Um, yep," Stringbean said, blinking in surprise. "You know her?"

"More or less," Mila answered. "Go on."

"Elana and her mom were having a garage sale. Elana wanted me to come over to get something," Stringbean explained. "It was the falcon, of course."

"Of course." I nodded.

I poured myself another grape juice.

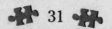 31

"I went over there in the morning," Stringbean explained, "just like Elana told me. She handed me the falcon and I left. It was easy."

"What about Elana's mother?" I asked. "Was she around?"

Stringbean looked to the clouds for an answer. "No, now that I think about it," he said. "Elana said she needed a hairbrush or something. Her mother went inside to get

it. That's when Elana wrapped up the falcon and gave it to me."

"Didn't all this, um, seem strange to you?" Mila asked.

Stringbean looked away, thinking. Finally he admitted, "Yes, it was strange. I didn't feel right about it. But Elana asked me to do it, and she doesn't like the word *no*."

"I've noticed," Mila commented. "So you're cousins, huh?"

"Cousins, or second cousins," Stringbean answered vaguely. "Something like that."

"What about the brother?" I asked. "It's his falcon, isn't it?"

"No. I mean, Elana didn't say it was," Stringbean said, scratching his head.

"Tell me about Elana's brother," I repeated. "What's he like? Is he close with Elana?"

Stringbean laughed. "Are you kidding?! They fight like cats and dogs. He's in high school. He's the star of the soccer team. I like him. And he loves torturing Elana." Stringbean paused, then grinned. "I think maybe that's why I like him."

I glanced at my notes. "So there's a falcon missing and you need it found."

"And fast," Stringbean said. "Elana will flip if she finds out I lost it."

"She doesn't know?" Mila asked.

"That's the strange thing," Stringbean replied. "Elana was supposed to come by last night to pick it up."

"Yeah, and . . . ?"

"And . . . she never showed," Stringbean said. "Lucky me, huh?"

"Maybe not so lucky after all." I tilted my head to an empty glass jar. "You still owe me a dollar."

Chapter Six
The Plot Thickens

Stringbean filled us in on a few more details. He paid up, and we walked him to the front of the house.

I grabbed his shoulder before he left. "Promise me, Stringbean," I said. "That story of yours is true, right?"

Stringbean held up a hand in the Boy Scout's pledge. "On my honor," he said. "Every word. If you don't believe me, just ask Elana. Or ask Bobby Solofsky. He saw me at the garage sale."

"Solofsky?" Mila said, her eyes widening. "*He* was there?"

Stringbean nodded. "I guess he knows Elana, too. They were talking together when I got there."

I could almost hear the wheels turning in Mila's head.

The minute Stringbean left, Mila gave me a sharp elbow to the ribs. "Jigsaw," she said. "I asked Solofsky point-blank. He said he was nowhere near that garage sale on Sunday."

I rolled my eyes. "Imagine that. Bobby Solofsky is lying. That's the first thing about this case that *doesn't* surprise me."

"Solofsky must be involved somehow," Mila concluded. "Why else would he lie?"

"I can always tell when Solofsky is lying," I told her. "His lips move."

"One thing keeps bugging me," Mila added.

"What's that?"

"This nutty falcon!" Mila exclaimed. She counted off on her fingers. "What's so special about a statue of a falcon? Why does it turn everyone into a liar?"

Mila crossed her arms, rocking back and forth. She hummed softly, then sang:

"The facts came marching one by one,
    hurrah, hurrah!
The facts came marching one by one,
    hurrah, hurrah!
The facts came marching one by one.

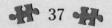 37

We'll solve this mystery before we're done!
And they all were lying about . . . a falcon . . .
But why? — I don't know — boom, boom, boom!"

"Well, at least now we've got two new characters in our story," I said to Mila. "Stringbean Noonan and Bobby Solofsky."

Mila grinned. "Yes. And the plot has taken an interesting turn." Mila checked her watch. "It's almost time for dinner. Let's go have a quick chat with Elana Wonderly."

"Let's," I agreed. "She's got some explaining to do."

We found Elana Wonderly lying on a hammock in her backyard. A tall glass of

lemonade, complete with a straw and a little umbrella, sat on a clear glass outdoor table. An American Girl catalog lay across her chest. She peered at us through daisy-shaped sunglasses.

"Jigsaw," she cooed. "What a nice surprise."

"I've had a few surprises myself," I said. "But I wouldn't call them nice. I just had a talk with your cousin Stringbean Noonan. You remember him, don't you? Tall, skinny kid. Seems to like falcons."

Elana pushed the sunglasses up into her hair. Her cheeks pinkened, then turned pale. She stammered, "I . . . I can . . . explain everything."

"I'm sure you can," I clucked.

Elana blinked twice. She dabbed her eyes with the tips of her fingers. "Well, um, it's not what it looks like. I mean . . . um . . . it's not what you think."

"Enough with the lies," I complained. "Try telling the truth this time."

Chapter Seven

The Black Falcon

Elana Wonderly slowly stood up, stretching her slender arms skyward. She sipped on the lemonade. And sat down on the grass beside a plastic pink flamingo.

"Jigsaw," she finally said, "and . . ." Elana looked at Mila as if seeing her for the first time. "I forget your name," she teased. "What is it again? Mylar? Mildred?"

"It's Mila," my partner replied sharply.

"Oh, Mila. How sweet," Elana cooed. "What are you? The little helper?"

"She's my partner," I shot back. "We've had enough of your games, Elana. Come on, Mila. Let's go. We don't have to listen to this."

It took three steps before Elana Wonderly called us back.

Like I knew she would.

Sure, she pulled on her lip. She chewed up a couple of fingernails. She ran her fingers through her thick red hair. The whole nine yards. And finally, *finally,* she

started talking. "I've been bad," Elana admitted, her green eyes locked on mine. "Sometimes very, very bad. I've always been that way, for as long as I can remember."

I stood silent, my face blank.

"My brother is Willie Wonderly," she told us, a strange smile on her face. "The soccer star. Oh, Willie is perfect in every way. Handsome, strong. A great athlete. A good student. A hero." She paused, and her eyes narrowed darkly. "He's also the meanest, cruelest brother on the face of this earth."

"That breaks my heart," I said. "Really, it does. But what does it have to do with the falcon?"

Elana scowled. "You're not being very nice."

I sighed. "No, maybe not. But I'm tired. My brain hurts. My knees itch. And you haven't said one word of the truth since I met you."

Elana nodded, curling her lips into a satisfied smile. "Yes, I probably deserved that. You're awfully smart, aren't you?"

I sighed.

"The falcon," prodded Mila.

"Ah, yes. The falcon," Elana said. "It's my brother's. The wonderful Willie Wonderly. He's a wonder, all right. There's something inside that falcon that I want."

"Like what?" Mila asked.

"A slip of paper," Elana answered. "The combination to his safe is written on it."

I sat down on the grass on the other side of the flamingo. "So you cooked up this little plot," I said. "Just to get the falcon."

Elana smiled. "Brilliant, aren't I?"

Mila made a face. "Why not just take it yourself?"

"You don't know my brother," Elana answered. "He'd know, and he'd come looking for me. No, I had to be more clever than that."

"Okay, sure," I countered. "So you asked your cousin Stringbean to do you a favor. You knew he'd do it, too. You're used to people doing what you want."

Elana's eyes twinkled. "*Most* people," she answered. "I'm not sure about you."

I wasn't sure, either. So I let that one pass without taking a swing at it. "Then you told Stringbean to hide it in the hole of a tree. One small problem, though." I paused, watching her carefully. "Now the falcon is gone."

Elana's mouth opened slightly. She raised her eyebrows. And blinked. Twice.

"But you knew that already," I continued. "That's why you never followed up with Stringbean. You knew he didn't have the falcon anymore. You knew it had been taken from the tree. Isn't that right?"

Bull's-eye. That time I got to her.

I could tell by the way she suddenly stopped chewing her lip.

So I decided to take another shot.

"And that's where Bobby Solofsky enters our story." I held up a hand. "Stop me if you know how this ends."

Elana picked at a fingernail. She looked at me with troubled eyes. "Oh, that's just the beginning, Jigsaw. Because the funny thing is, I'm the one who's been double-crossed."

Chapter Eight
Double-crossed

Between sips of lemonade, Elana explained that she hired Bobby Solofsky to steal the falcon back from Stringbean.

"Huh?" Mila asked.

"Solofsky is a detective, too," Elana said. "Cheap. He only charged me fifty cents."

"And Solofsky isn't exactly honest," I commented. "So he had no problem doing your dirty work."

Elana's green eyes looked unhappily into mine. "Anyway, he was supposed to follow Stringbean, then take the falcon from the tree and give it back to me later that day."

"And that's when you got double-crossed?" Mila asked.

"He never came back with the falcon," Elana admitted. "I waited, but he never showed up. When I called him on the phone, he pretended I had the wrong number. He talked in a squeaky voice and acted like an old lady from Bulgaria. What a weirdo."

My head was spinning. "Okay," I said. "I think I get it. You gave Stringbean the falcon.

Then you hired Solofsky — cheap — to take it back. Why?"

Elana frowned. "I was worried about Stringbean. He's such a scaredy cat. I wasn't sure he could keep a secret." She laughed out loud. "Stringbean probably thinks it's all *his fault*!"

I didn't see what was so funny.

"What's Solofsky's game?" I wondered out loud.

"Maybe he decided to keep the falcon for himself," Mila suggested.

Maybe, I thought. Or maybe blackmail was on his mind. Elana would pay a lot more than fifty cents to get that falcon back. Maybe Solofsky figured that out.

It was getting late. My stomach rumbled, telling me it was dinnertime. "Well, you paid us five dollars to find a falcon. So we'll find the falcon for you . . . tomorrow."

"What if Solofsky says he doesn't have it?" Elana wondered. "That kid is trouble."

"I don't mind a little bit of trouble," I murmured. "But I do mind missing dinner. We'll call you tomorrow."

Chapter Nine

Building a Character

In school on Tuesday, I made sure that Solofsky was going to be home that afternoon. But I didn't tell him that Mila and I were planning to visit. I wanted it to be a surprise.

Ms. Gleason read the book *Wemberly Worried* by Kevin Henkes. We listened on the reading rug while munching on our morning snacks.

Wemberly Worried was a story about a mouse named Wemberly who worried about everything. Even nutty stuff like

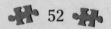

rusty swings and cracks in walls. Then she had to go to her first day of school — and she worried a lot more.

When Ms. Gleason finished reading, we talked about the story. Ms. Gleason was big on "book talks." Our class spent more time talking about books than we did reading them.

Go figure.

"This story is about character," Ms. Gleason said. "The writer makes Wemberly come alive for us by creating details. Wemberly has a spot over her eye. She likes stripes. She always carries around a stuffed animal named Petal."

"And she worries too much!" added Athena Lorenzo.

Ms. Gleason smiled. "Yes, that is Wemberly's problem. When you think about it, most stories are like that. The main character often has a problem to solve," she explained. "The problem could

be anything. Maybe someone is afraid of thunder. Maybe a character is locked in a tower by a wicked king."

"Maybe a character needs to solve a mystery," Mila suggested.

Ms. Gleason suddenly tilted her head. She held up a finger, listening. There was a strange noise . . . coming from . . . Joey Pignattano! Joey had his head on the floor. I'd say he was staring at the ceiling, but his eyes were closed.

"Is Joey . . . snoring?" Ms. Gleason asked Ralphie Jordan.

Ralphie smiled, bright and wide, like always. "That's my problem," he said, clamping his hands over his ears. "Joey snores too loud!"

We all giggled, and that seemed to wake up Joey. He jolted up, eyes wide, and shouted, "Pancakes!"

We laughed even louder.

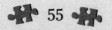

Joey blushed, looking around the room. "I guess I was having a dream," he sheepishly confessed.

"Yeah, about pancakes!" snorted Helen Zuckerman.

Ms. Gleason had us do some waking-up exercises, like touching our toes and wiggling our arms. Then we returned to our desks and took out our writing folders.

"Let's try to create a character together,"

Ms. Gleason said. She picked up a piece of chalk. "Bobby, name an animal."

"A falcon!" Solofsky answered.

I raised an eyebrow.

"A lost falcon!" Stringbean added.

"Very good detail, Jasper," Ms. Gleason said. "I'm already curious about this lost falcon. See how the details make a character seem real to us." She looked around the room. "Come on, boys and girls. Think like writers. Tell me more about this falcon."

"It's name is Elana," I called out.

Bobby turned and glared at me. His nose wrinkled, like a rat who smelled something he didn't like.

"Where do falcons live?" Ms. Gleason asked. "What do they usually eat?"

"North Dakota!"

"Mice!"

"Pizza!"

Ms. Gleason laughed. "Pizza!? I like that

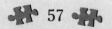

idea. Elana the lost falcon likes pizza. Or maybe she just wants to taste pizza."

"She's sick of mice!" Ralphie called out.

"And she can't fly!" Danika Starling added.

"Okay, okay," Ms. Gleason said happily. "I can see that we've got a lot of enthusiastic thinkers in room 201. Now I'd like you to take the next few minutes to outline your own character. Don't worry about writing a whole story. We'll try that later in the year.

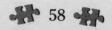

Jot down some words in your journals. Add details that will help us 'see' your character." She shrugged. "Who knows? Maybe an idea for a story will pop through!"

Chapter Ten
Solofsky

Tall evergreens lined the stone path to Bobby Solofsky's house. I pushed the doorbell. Mila and I waited. And nobody answered, right on time. Suddenly — "YAH!" — a loud scream startled us.

"Bwaaa-ha-ha!" Bobby Solofsky jumped out of the bushes and howled. He pointed at us, held his belly, and laughed. "Tricked you! Tricked you!" he sang.

Yeesh.

I hate it when he does that.

"Hiding in bushes, Solofsky. That's

swell," I groaned. "But let's stop fooling around. Mila and I came here on business."

Solofsky slid a tongue across his teeth. A sucking sound came from his mouth. That is, I *think* it was his mouth.

"What do you want with me?" Solofsky answered. "I didn't do nothing."

"Do anything," Mila corrected.

Solofsky scowled.

"We've got questions," I said. "We're looking for answers."

"Try the library," Solofsky replied.

I looked toward his house. "Are you going to invite us in?"

Solofsky shrugged. "Yeah, sure, why not? Nobody's home except my sister, Karla. She's probably sending Instant Messages on the computer."

Solofsky led us into his living room. He slumped onto the couch and threw his feet onto the table. He said, "I knew you'd show up, Jones. You gave enough hints in class today."

I stood across from him, glancing around the room. "Yeah," I remembered, ". . . *a lost falcon named Elana.*"

"Speaking of falcons," Mila said. "Where is it, Solofsky?"

Solofsky stared at the tops of his sneakers. He lifted an arm. Without bothering to look up, he pointed a lazy finger across the room.

And there it was.

The black falcon.

It was inside an old bookcase that had fancy glass doors.

"Great," I said. "We'll take it and get out of here."

"No, you won't," Solofsky stated.

"Oh?"

"You won't," he said, "because you can't. But don't be mad. I can't, either."

Mila took a step forward. "Explain," she ordered.

"That display case is locked," Solofsky said. "But that's not the worst part."

We waited for the worst part to come.

It came.

With a thud.

Solofsky sat up to explain. "After I got the falcon from the tree, I came right home.

The falcon was wrapped in fancy paper. I must have put it on the dining room table. Then I went to my room."

"Yeah, so?"

"So, Sunday was my mom's birthday," Solofsky told us. "When she saw the package, she thought I'd left her a birthday present."

"She opened it?" Mila asked in surprise.

"You should have heard her," Solofsky said. "My mom nearly squeezed me to death. She was so happy. She said it was the nicest thing I ever did for her."

I jerked a thumb toward the bookcase. "Your mom thinks this falcon . . ."

". . . which you STOLE . . ." Mila added.

". . . is the nicest birthday present you ever gave her?" I asked.

Solofsky nodded unhappily. "Yup."

Mila pulled on her long black hair. "Well," she decided, "you have to tell your mother the truth."

Solofsky didn't look up.

"Right?" Mila insisted.

"Wrong," Solofsky said. "See, I forgot it was my mother's birthday. I didn't have a present for her or nothing. But that falcon saved my life. And it made my mom happy."

He walked to the bookcase, bent down, and stared through the glass at the falcon. "I can't take this falcon away from her. Even if I *could* get it out of this locked bookcase. And I can't. So I won't."

Solofsky turned to look at us. He crossed his arms and stood with his legs wide. "Forget it, Jigsaw. The falcon stays here."

Chapter Eleven
The Key

"Solofsky," I said. "You're absolutely right."

"He is?" Mila asked in surprise.

"I am?" Bobby wondered.

"Yes, the falcon stays here. For now, at least," I said. "Until we can figure this out."

I paced back and forth, my hands deep in my pockets. Mila rocked back and forth on her toes, humming softly. We thought and thought.

Finally, I stopped. "I don't want to take the falcon, Bobby. But I have to look at it."

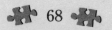

Bobby pulled on the glass door. "I told you. It's locked."

"There must be a key around here somewhere," I mused.

Mila asked Bobby for a hairpin. "Maybe your sister Karla has one," she suggested.

"What for?" Bobby asked.

"I might be able to pick the lock," Mila said. "I've seen it done on television lots of times."

While Mila fooled with the lock, I scanned the room. Where would Bobby's mother keep the key? I searched through desk drawers and underneath houseplants. I looked up at the tall bookcase, wondering.

"Your mom is tall, right?" I asked Solofsky. He nodded.

"Bring me that chair," I told him.

I climbed on an armchair and stood on my tippy-toes. I reached up and blindly felt the ledge with my fingers. After a few seconds, I stepped down.

I was holding a key.

The falcon was smooth and surprisingly heavy. It was mounted on a wooden base. I turned it over in my hands. I grew worried. How could a piece of paper be inside? "There's no opening," I complained. "No slot. Nothing."

"Let me see," Mila asked. She held the falcon under a table lamp. She pulled out a magnifying glass. Bobby and I peered over her shoulders.

"Hmmmm," she finally said.

"Hmmmm?" I echoed.

Bobby whispered in my ear, "Is that a good 'Hmmmm' or a bad 'Hmmmm'?"

Mila pressed her thumbs against the wooden base. She tried twisting it and flipping it. Nothing happened. Then, by accident, she pushed the falcon's beak.

And — *boing* — the wooden base slid open.

"Aha!" Mila squealed with delight. "The

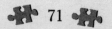

beak must have triggered a spring mechanism!"

"Uh-huh," Bobby mumbled. "What she said."

Mila poked a finger inside the falcon and pulled out a piece of paper. She handed it to me.

"Secret code," I muttered.

Solofsky snatched the falcon back from Mila. "Hey, take it easy, Solofsky," I

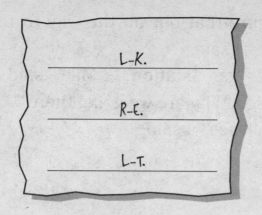

_____ L-K. _____

_____ R-E. _____

_____ L-T. _____

demanded. "I already said you can keep the falcon . . . for now."

Mila said, "Let's go see Elana Wonderly."

I shook my head. "Not yet, Mila. There's something I've got to do first."

We headed out the door. Solofsky held the falcon in one hand and waved good-bye with the other.

I handed the secret code to Mila. "See if you

can figure that out on the way to the gas station," I said.

"The gas station?" Mila said with surprise. "Why are we going there?"

"You'll see," I said.

Chapter Twelve
Opening the Safe

I have three older brothers and one older sister. It isn't always easy being the youngest in my family. My brothers call me Worm and Shorty. But there are nice things about being the youngest, too.

My oldest brother, Billy, is pretty cool. He works part-time in a gas station after school and on weekends. He helps me out sometimes. Like yesterday, for example.

Mila and I went to Billy's gas station. I asked if he knew Willie Wonderly. Billy said

that he did. Then I asked him to do me a favor. And Billy said, "No problem, Worm. What do you need?"

So last night he made a phone call to Willie Wonderly.

And my plan was set.

It was as easy as swatting a fly.

Mila and I went to Elana Wonderly's house on Wednesday afternoon. Elana met us in the doorway. "Do you have the combination?" she asked.

I handed it to her and waited.

"I don't understand," she said.

"It's a code," Mila explained.

"We'll tell you what it means," I said. "If you let us be there when you open the safe."

Elana didn't have much choice. She led us upstairs into her brother's room. It was large, with slanted ceilings that were covered with soccer posters. Trophies filled a wall shelf.

I took the paper from Elana.

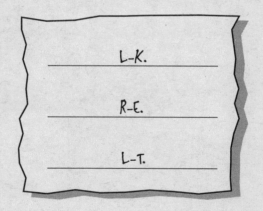

_____ L–K.

_____ R–E.

_____ L–T.

"It's the combination," I said. "But it's in code. I guess your brother doesn't trust you."

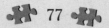

Elana tapped her foot impatiently.

"The L and R and L are easy," Mila said. "After all, it's a combination: Left, Right, Left."

"Then there's the other part, K and E and T," I noted. "We figure it's a substitution code. Each letter stands for a number."

Elana, the princess, still looked confused. I guessed detective work wasn't her bag.

"The letter A would be the number 1," I said. "B would be 2. C is 3, and so on through the alphabet." I grabbed a pen and wrote on the paper:

Left 11
Right 5
Left 20

Elana quickly went to Willie's safe. He kept it inside his closet behind a bunch of boxes. Mila and I watched, amused, when she opened the safe . . . and pulled out a single piece of loose-leaf paper.

Elana read the note, glared at me angrily, and threw it to the floor. She looked about ready to explode. Mila picked up the paper. I read it over her shoulder. It was a note to Elana from her brother, Willie.

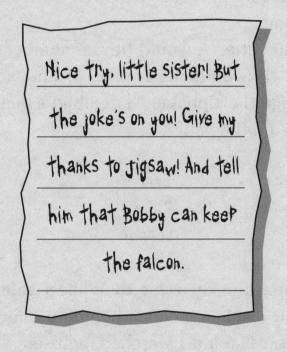

Nice try, little sister! But the joke's on you! Give my thanks to Jigsaw! And tell him that Bobby can keep the falcon.

Chapter Thirteen
Honesty

Elana stared at me with hot green eyes. "Give my thanks to Jigsaw," she repeated. "What did you do, Jones?"

"Something that you'll never understand," I said. "But I'll try to explain it to you."

Elana sat down on the edge of Willie's bed.

"You don't have any grape juice, do you?" I asked.

Elana's eyes narrowed darkly. I took that as a no.

"I'm a detective," I began. "It's good work and I like it. Sometimes it gets a little dirty. I have to follow people. Or search through their stuff, looking for clues," I said.

Elana didn't move.

"But there are certain things I won't do," I told her. "I won't lie, and I won't steal."

"But I paid you five dollars," Elana insisted.

I nodded, glancing at Mila. "Yes, you did," I replied. "And five dollars buys a lot of things. But it doesn't buy me."

I took an envelope out of my pocket and tossed it on her lap. "There's your money," I said. "All of it."

Elana's jaw dropped open. "I don't get it, Jones."

"I didn't think you would," I answered. "You can't buy my honesty, Elana. It's not for sale. I'm a detective, remember. In the end, the truth is all I've got. I won't help you steal."

"Why not?" Elana asked.

I sighed. "Look," I explained. "I brush my teeth twice a day. I always look in the mirror when I do it. The thing is, I want to like the guy I'm looking at. You can't turn me into a thief."

Mila spoke up. "Jigsaw called Willie last night," she explained. "He told him everything."

Elana's cheeks turned white. And her green eyes — those amazing, beautiful, sparkling eyes — turned dull and blank.

"I told him to empty out his safe, and fast," I said.

The room was silent for a long time. We all stood staring at one another. Elana fingered the envelope in her lap.

"You and your brother have problems," I told Elana. "Big problems. He's a soccer star. And maybe you're jealous." I shrugged. "You say he's mean to you. Maybe you deserve it. Maybe you don't."

I continued. "You two should try to make things better," I said. "You're family — and families shouldn't treat one another this way."

This time, real tears filled Elana's eyes, then spilled down her face. She whispered softly, "But . . . where do we even begin?" she asked.

"Start with the truth," I said.

Elana didn't answer. She just stared at her hands unhappily.

After a while, Mila finally said, "Let's go, Jigsaw."

So I pulled my hat down on my head, nice and tight.

I turned my back on Elana Wonderly.

And I walked out of the room, and out of the house, and out of her life, forever.

My head was held high.

Chapter Fourteen
My Story

Later that week, I sat down at my kitchen table. I had to write a story for school. Ms. Gleason told us it didn't have to be long. We didn't even have to finish it. She only wanted us to try putting words down on paper. I chomped on the eraser of my pencil.

One day, I decided, I was going to invent a watermelon-flavored pencil eraser.

But for now, I thought about character, and setting, and plot. I thought about the case. How it all started when I was at my desk in the basement, doing a jigsaw

puzzle. I remembered the fly buzzing around the room. I remembered the phone call from Elana Wonderly.

I poured myself a tall glass of grape juice.

And started writing . . .

There's a hand-lettered sign behind an old desk in my basement. It reads: **JIGSAW JONES, PRIVATE EYE.** I solve mysteries. . . .

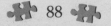

Puzzling Codes
and
Activities

Find That Falcon!

Bobby Solofsky has hidden the black falcon somewhere in this maze. Can you help Jigsaw and Mila find it?

start

finish

Answer on page 101.

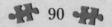

Test Your Detective Skills!

Good detectives like Jigsaw Jones have to pay close attention to everything that goes on around them. This is called being observant. Are you ready to practice your powers of observation? Before you read the questions below, turn to pages 10–11. Now look at the picture for fifteen seconds. Ask a friend or family member to time you. Then see if you can answer the questions below. But don't look back at the picture. That would be cheating!

1. How many people are in the picture?
2. Can you see a dog or a cat in the picture?
3. What is Elana sitting on?
4. Can you see the house in this picture?
5. What is the girl inside the garage looking at?
6. What is on Elana's shirt?

Answers on page 101.

Puzzling Pictures

Take a close look at these two pictures of Jigsaw in his office. There are five things that are not the same in both pictures. Can you spot the differences?

BONUS: A black falcon is hidden in the picture on the front cover of this book. Can you find it?

Answer on page 103.

Answers on page 101.

 93

Secret Codes and Jigsaw Puzzles

On pages 77–79 of *The Case of the Missing Falcon*, Elana Wonderly's brother uses a Substitution Code to keep the combination of his safe a secret. You can use the same Substitution Code to send top-secret messages to your friends.

Here's how it works: Each number stands for a letter in the alphabet. Number one is letter A. Number two is letter B. Number three is letter C and so on through the alphabet.

Use the Substitution Code to help Jigsaw and Mila figure out the secret question written below.

23 8 15   9 19   10 9 7 19 1 23' 19

23 15 18 19 20   5 14 5 13 25?

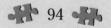

Now that you know the question, put together the jigsaw-puzzle pieces below to find the answer.

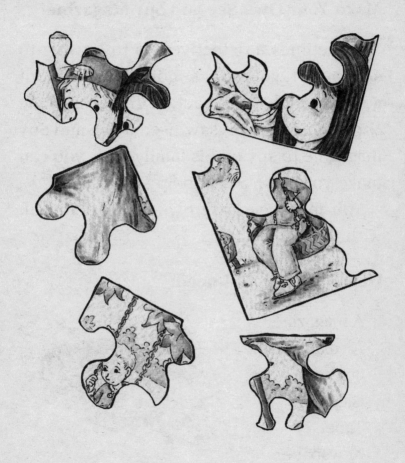

Answer on page 102.

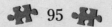 95

Detective Tips

Make Your Own See-and-Spy Magazine!

Sometimes a detective has to be able to see and hear what's going on without getting caught in the act. In *The Case of the Secret Valentine*, Jigsaw used a See-and-Spy magazine to spy on his family. Now you can make your own See-and-Spy magazine!

You may need a grown-up to help you with this project.

Here's what you'll need:

A magazine
A small mirror
Scissors
Glue
Tape
Newspaper
Wet paper towels

1. First lay out the newspaper so the table doesn't get sticky.

2. Then open the magazine to the inside back cover. Squirt a few globs of glue on the pages.

3. Next smush the last page of the magazine to the inside back cover. Glue might leak out the edges. Use the wet paper towels to wipe it up.

4. Wait for the glue to dry. Then cut a peephole the size of a quarter into the side of the magazine you just glued.

5. On the opposite page, tape a small mirror to the magazine.

6. Congratulations! You have finished your See-and-Spy magazine! Now sit down and hold the magazine up in front of your face. Pretend to read. You can peek through the hole to see what is happening in front of you. To see what is happening behind you, look in the mirror.

Write Your Own Mystery

In this book, Ms. Gleason's class learns a lot about writing mysteries. Use the fill-ins below to help think of ideas for your own story.

Characters. Who is in your story? _____

_____

Details. What are your characters like? Are they people or animals? Where do they live? What do they like to eat? _____

_____

Setting. Where does your story take place?

_____

Plot. What happens in your story? _____

_____

_____

_____

NEED A HINT? Flip back to Chapters Four and Nine to see what Ms. Gleason says about writing a story!

From the Top Secret Pages of Jigsaw Jones's Detective Journal

Now you can solve mysteries like Jigsaw Jones and Mila Yeh!

Case: The case of _____

Client: _____

Suspects: _____

_____

Clues: _____

_____

Key Words: _____

_____

Mystery Solved: _____

_____

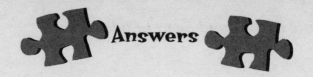

Answers

Find That Falcon!

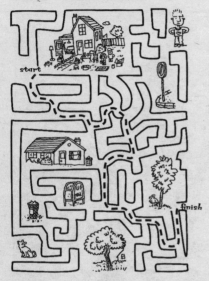

Test Your Detective Skills!

1. Eight
2. Yes, a cat.
3. A folding chair
4. Yes
5. Clothes
6. A daisy

Puzzling Pictures

Jigsaw Puzzle and Secret Code

Question: Who is Jigsaw's worst enemy?

Answer: Bobby Solofsky!

Bonus (from page 93):

MEET
Geronimo Stilton

A MOUSE WITH A NOSE FOR GREAT STORIES

Who is Geronimo Stilton? Why, that's me! I run a newspaper, but my true passion is writing tales of adventure. Here on Mouse Island, my books are all bestsellers! What's that? You've never read one? Well, my books are full of fun. They are whisker-licking-good stories, and that's a promise!

www.scholastic.com/kids